THE TIME WARP TRIO

It's All Greek to Me

by Jon Scieszka

illustrated by Lane Smith

SCHOLASTIC INC.
New York Toronto London Auckland Sydney
Mexico City New Delhi Hong Kong

ISBN 0-439-20731-2

12 11 10 9 8 7 6 5 4 3 2   1 2 3 4 5 6/0

Printed in the U.S.A.   40

First Scholastic printing, January 2001

Set in Sabon

To my daughter Casey and her fellow fourth grade
actors, music teacher Maggie Harth, and
director Debra Barsha for bringing gods
and goddesses, mortals and monsters to life on stage.

—J. S.

ONE

"Nice doggie, nice doggie, nice doggie," said Sam.

The monster barked three times—once with each of its three giant heads.

"A three-headed dog?" Fred pulled down his Yankees cap with a giant paper eye pinned on it. "You have got to be kidding."

The three heads snarled, showed fangs, and drooled and drooled and drooled. They didn't look like they were kidding.

"Down boy, down boy, down boy," said Sam to the dog. "Do something," said Sam to me.

Fred, Sam, and I backed against a cold wet rock. We checked what weapons we had to fight this beast. Sam held a lyre. Fred gripped his aluminum-foil-covered thunderbolt. And I was armed with one gold spray-painted plastic apple. That and our bed-sheet togas were all we had.

Screams and groans echoed in the dim mist all around us. I looked for some way around the growling mad demon dog. He was standing guard over the one and only path out.

"How the heck did this happen?" said Fred. "One minute we're about to go onstage for our school play, the next minute we're in hell."

"I believe it's called Hades, Cyclops head," said Sam. "Since I'm guessing that triple-headed drooler is Cerberus, guard dog of the ancient Greek underworld."

"But that's not real," said Fred. "That's just mythology stuff like in the play. And things like this only

happen when we mess with *The Book*. And Joe swore he locked that thing up. And—"

Cerberus barked madly.

"And Joe?" said Sam.

"Well I kind of . . ." I said.

"Joe?" said Fred.

"I sort of . . ."

"JOE?!" said Sam and Fred.

"Okay I stuck *The Book* in my backpack because Uncle Joe is coming to the show tonight and I was going to give it back to him but when Fred hit *The Book* and the script with the thunderbolt it must have set something off because that's when the green mist started," I blurted out in one breath.

Sam and Fred looked at me like they were going to kill me.

Cerberus, three-headed dog of Greek mythology, looked at us like he was definitely going to kill us *and* enjoy eating us.

"I wouldn't say you're a perfect idiot," said Sam. "Nobody's perfect."

The beast was so close we could see its six bloodshot eyes.

"Well, do one of those magic tricks you're

3

always talking about and get us out of here," said Fred.

I racked my brain for any good magic tricks for dogs.

"Sit!" I yelled. "Stay! Roll over! Play dead!"

Cerberus growled and stepped closer.

"Joe?" said Sam nervously. "I don't think this is working."

"This never fails," I said. I picked up a small rock and threw it into the gloomy mist. "Fetch!"

Not one of the three slobbering heads even turned to look.

One head locked its red eyes on Sam. One head stared at Fred. One head zeroed in on me. The thing was so close we could see each thick black hair raised on its back and smell each blast of its roadkill breath.

The last thing I remember thinking was: "What a way to go, eaten by a nasty-smelling monster that isn't even real."

TWO

I can just hear one of you smart guys out there saying, "How can you travel into Greek mythology? I thought *The Book* could only travel through time."

Honestly, I have no idea how we ended up facing the three-headed dog of the underworld from Greek mythology.

Well, I have some idea, but it wasn't really my fault.

Okay, it was kind of my fault, but I was only trying to get things back to normal by putting *The Book* back in Uncle Joe's hands.

See my life has been just too strange for words since my uncle Joe gave me this book for my birthday.

I'm sure you've got books for your birthday

before. But this book is like no other book before or since. It's a small book. A dark blue book with odd silver writing and symbols on it. It's a time-warping book.

And yes, I'll admit it. I have no idea how *The Book* works or how to control it. But I do know it's sent Fred, Sam, and me back to the Stone Age, forward to the future, and even into other books.

One thing that always stays the same is the green time-traveling mist that comes out of *The Book*. The other thing is that once we go somewhere, the only way we can get back is to find *The Book* in that new time or place.

Get it? Got it. Good.

Like I said, it wasn't my fault. But here's what I think happened:

Our whole grade was backstage in the school auditorium, five minutes before the first performance of our play *The Myth of Power*. It was a play about gods and goddesses and mortals and monsters and all that Greek mythology stuff we were studying in school. We had made some great sets of Mount Olympus (the mountain all the gods live on top of) and the underworld, Hades.

The music teacher was the director, so most of the play was about how music is the answer for everything. But we helped write a lot of the scenes, so all the gods and goddesses sounded like a bunch of wiseguys. We also got to make some excellent thunderbolts to throw around, and wrote in a lot of fight scenes for the monsters.

Anyway—that's why we were all standing around at school dressed up in bed-sheet togas. Fred was a one-eyed Cyclops, with an eye pinned on his Yankees hat. Sam was Orpheus, wandering around playing his lyre. I was Paris, the good-looking guy who has to decide which goddess is the fairest and give her the golden apple.

While we waited, Sam was rereading his *Book of Snappy Insults* for the millionth time. We had been using all the good ones for the past month, and even managed to get a few in the play. Fred was pacing, trying to remember all two of his lines. And I think that's when it happened.

"Help me out, Joe," said Fred. "David says, 'Hey you guys—look!' Then do I say, 'We made those thunderbolts'? Or does Charlie say his line first?"

"Cyclops Fred," said Sam, "if you had to live by your wits, you'd starve."

Fred picked up an aluminum-foil-covered thunderbolt and bopped Sam on the head with it.

I took my script out of my backpack. "Here it is. David says, 'Hey you guys—look!' Charlie says, 'Our thunderbolts.' *Then* your line is, 'We made those thunderbolts.'" I stuffed the script back into my backpack.

"Something is preying on your mind, Fred," said Sam. "But don't worry. It will die of starvation."

Fred swung his thunderbolt again. Sam ducked. Fred missed. The thunderbolt hit my backpack. Something glowed weirdly for a second inside my backpack. Then my pack started leaking green mist.

I saw the house lights go black. I heard the piano playing the beginning of the first musical number. Our Greek myth play was starting. And Fred, Sam, and I were swirling off in a green mist time tornado farther and stranger than we'd ever gone before.

THREE

Cerberus crouched, ready to spring.

Fred held up his aluminum-foil thunderbolt. Sam tried to hide behind his lyre.

"That's it!" I yelled.

"No kidding, this is it," said Sam. "I just never thought I'd die in a bed-sheet toga."

"No, you can save us," I said. "Just like in the play. Remember? Orpheus puts Cerberus to sleep with music from his lyre."

"There's just one small difference," said Sam. "In the play I'm putting to sleep Ben with two extra stuffed dog heads coming out of his sweatshirt. Here I'm putting to sleep . . . A LIVE MAD DROOLING GROWLING MONSTER!!!"

Fred looked desperate. "Well this aluminum-foil thunderbolt isn't going to do much for us. Why don't you give it a try? What have we got to lose?"

Sam cradled his lyre and nervously plucked a few strings.

Cerberus froze, then cocked one head to listen.

Sam plucked the beginning of "Twinkle, Twinkle, Little Star."

Cerberus sat down. Now all three heads were beginning to listen.

"I think it's working," I whispered.

Sam finished "Twinkle, Twinkle" and started again.

One head growled.

Sam kept playing.

Two heads growled.

"He doesn't want to hear that song again," said Fred.

"It's the only song I know," whispered Sam frantically. He began another round of "Twinkle, Twinkle."

All three heads growled.

"Wait a minute. I've got the real answer," said Fred digging into a pocket under his Cyclops costume.

Sam started "Twinkle, Twinkle" for a fourth time.

11

Cerberus howled, opened his jaws, and jumped forward to snap Sam in one mad gulp. Sam fell back. Fred tossed the thing from his pocket. The middle head chomped it in half and stopped in midair.

Half a piece of chocolate cake fell from the middle head's mouth. The left head sniffed it. The right head bit it. Then all three heads were snapping at each other, fighting for the last chunk of cake.

"My last Ding Dong," said Fred. "Now let's make a break for it."

No one had to tell us twice. We ran up the path past Cerberus, who was busy snarling, fighting, and biting himself. We ran past a guy rolling a huge rock up a hill. We ran past another guy reaching for fruit and water that kept moving away. We ran past spooky shadows and sights that we didn't want to see, until we finally burst above ground into the sweet green grass and beautiful hot sunshine.

"Yikes," huffed Sam. "I take back every bad thing I ever said about you, Fred. That Ding Dong was a stroke of pure genius."

We lay back on the grass and soaked up the sun,

trying to catch our breath and shake off the creepy cold and gloom of the underworld.

"So once again, let me guess," said Sam, squinting through his glasses up at the clouds. "We've lost *The Book* and will never get home unless we find it."

"Well . . . yeah," I said.

"I've seen better heads on cabbage," said Insult Master Sam.

"And as usual, we have no idea where it is," said Fred.

"Well . . . yeah," I said. "But now we know it's not down in Hades. And since I think *The Book* has somehow sent us into our own play and the Greek myths all mixed together, the only other place it can be is Mount Olympus."

"Great," said Fred. "And with our luck, I'll bet the god who has it is probably the biggest, meanest, and strongest one of the bunch."

"Zeus," said Sam, squinting into the clouds.

"Yep, king of the gods on Mount Olympus," I said.

"Zeus," said Sam.

"So how do we get up there?" said Fred.

"Zeus!" said Sam lifting his arm.

"Okay, okay, we know the guy's name already," said Fred. "How do we find him?"

"Zeus! Zeus! Zeus!" croaked Sam, pointing to the clouds.

The shadow of a giant eagle suddenly covered us from above. With a whoosh of feathers and a burst of light the monster bird changed into a huge white-bearded god standing right in front of us. He pointed one threatening finger at us.

"YOU!" he thundered.

"Zeus?" we said.

FOUR

"**Y**OU," boomed Zeus in a voice that blew the hair straight back from our heads. "*YOU* STOLE MY THUNDERBOLTS!"

Sam and I stood frozen like statues.

Fred lifted up his aluminum-foil-covered thunderbolt. "This? Aw, this is just—"

"HEY! WATCH WHERE YOU'RE POINTING THAT THING!" yelled Zeus.

Fred faked throwing the thunderbolt. Zeus ducked again. I could almost see the lightbulb of an idea go on in Fred's head. "Yeah, we have your thunderbolt, and we're looking to trade."

"Ah, you Cyclopses are such a pain," said Zeus. "I try to help you and this is how you repay me? Ai yi yi." Zeus sat down on a nearby boulder. He squinted at Fred. "And what kind of Cyclops are

15

you anyway? I've never seen a Cyclops with three eyes."

"Three eyes?" said Fred. Then he felt the one eye taped to his Yankees cap. "Oh right. Well I . . . uhh . . ."

"Never mind," I said. "We are looking for a small blue book. Have you seen such a thing?"

Zeus turned his fiery gray eyes on me. "And who are you to speak, puny mortal? And where did you get the bad-fitting toga and strange sandals?"

I tried to adjust my bed-sheet toga and look noble in my sneakers. "I'm Joe . . . uh . . . Paris." I said. "I'm the Cyclops' agent. And we're looking to trade thunderbolts for *The Book*."

Zeus held his head in his hands. "Lost thunderbolts, nasty Cyclopses, greedy mortals—what a day. But if Hera finds out my thunderbolts are lost, I'm sunk."

Fred, Sam, and I looked at each other. This was getting scary. This wasn't the all-powerful Zeus you read about in Greek myths. This guy was the goofy, thunderbolt-losing Zeus from our play.

We couldn't believe it. Our own characters from the play had come to life. Then, just like in Act 2, we heard a screeching female voice from above.

16

"Zeus? Zeus, is that you down there?"

It was a line right from the play, but it wasn't Sara speaking it.

Zeus jumped to his feet. "It's Hera, my wife. She can't find out that my thunderbolts are gone. If she knows, everyone will know. What a blabbermouth. You've got to help me. Get rid of her."

I still didn't know how *The Book* had managed to bring our twisted version of Greek mythology to life. But I did know the only way to get out.

"Then will you help us find *The Book?*" I asked.

"Book, papyrus, tablet . . . whatever you want," said Zeus. "Just get rid of her." Zeus dove behind the boulder.

A gorgeous woman leading a peacock appeared from behind a tree.

"Hera?" I said.

"No, I'm the meter maid," said Hera sarcastically. "Now where is that bum, Zeus? I know I heard him thundering around down here. Where is he? Answer me. Are you paying attention?"

"I did once, but it wouldn't pay me back," said Sam.

Hera turned on Sam, widening her eyes, looking like she was going to fry him on the spot. I knew Sam had gone too far trying one of his insults on a goddess. Now it didn't matter where *The Book* was. We were all doomed to be burned like toast.

Hera raised one arm, pointed at Sam, and burst out laughing.

"Now that's the funniest thing I've heard one of you mortals say in a long time," said Hera, still laughing. "Your kind usually just shrivels up and goes dumb when I speak to you. Maybe you can help me out."

"We'd love to help you out," said Sam. "Which way did you come in?"

"One of us is crazy. But don't worry, I'll keep your secret," answered Hera with her own insult.

"Where have you been all my life? And when

are you going back there?" countered Sam.

Hera gave another laugh. "How can I miss you when you won't go away?"

Sam grinned. "I never forget a face, but in your case I'll make an exception."

Hera howled, laughing so hard she was crying.

Sam added another. "You have a face like a baby, and a mind to match."

Fred and I were cracking up.

"Stop, stop," said Hera, tears of laughter running down her face. "I give up. Who are you? I see you are a follower of the goddess of victory."

"Huh?" said Sam.

"You wear her name on your sandals—Nike."

"Oh, right," said Sam. "I'm Sam Orpheus, follower of Nike. That's Fred Cyclops, worshiper of Reebok. And that's Joe Paris, nuts over Fila."

Hera looked us over. "I don't think I know Reebok or Fila. Hmmm. Well, no matter. I was going to turn you all into poisonous little mushrooms for insulting me and stopping me from finding Zeus. But forget that old windbag."

The rock Zeus was hiding behind gave a little rumble.

"You should come up to the feast on Mount Olympus. We always need fresh entertainment. Bring your thunderbolt. And what is that you have there, young man?"

"It's a golden apple, ma'am . . . er, your goddess-ness," I stammered.

"And who is it for?" asked Hera.

I tried to shut Fred up because I knew what he was going to say, and I knew it could only mean trouble for me. But I couldn't stop him.

"It's for the fairest," blurted out Fred.

"For *me?* You shouldn't have," said Hera. "Now you *must* come up to Mount Olympus."

My head was spinning. In the last half hour we had gone from starting our school play to Hades to being invited to Mount Olympus. If things kept going anything like our play, I could guess what was going to happen if I went up to Mount Olympus with just one apple addressed to "The Fairest." All the gods and goddesses would fight over it and blame me.

"C'mon Joe, let's go," said Fred. "You said it yourself. *The Book* is probably up on Mount Olympus."

"On second thought, I'm sure there's no blue book up there," I said, trying desperately to think of a good excuse to not go up to Mount Olympus.

"The blue book?" said Hera. "Why of course we have it. I use it all the time."

"All right," said Sam. "So let's make like a tree and leaf."

Hera laughed. "Let's make like a deck of cards and shuffle off."

"We really shouldn't," I said, still trying to think of why we shouldn't, when I heard a sound that instantly changed my mind.

It was a sound I had suggested to end Act 1 of the play. It was the sound of marching feet, one voice calling, the others answering:

We are monsters, we are tough.
WE ARE MONSTERS, WE ARE TOUGH.
We don't take nobody's guff.
WE DON'T TAKE NOBODY'S GUFF.
Sound off!
MON—STERS!
Say it again!
MON—STERS!

21

Bring it on down!
**MONSTERS MONSTERS MONSTERS
WE RULE!**

It was the sound of Typhon, the hundred-dragon-headed boss of the monsters, leading a nightmare collection of bad guys from Greek mythology looking for a fight. It had seemed like a funny idea when we wrote the play. Now it didn't seem quite so funny.

The tramp of feet grew louder. I thought about what would happen when Typhon, snake-haired Medusa, the half-man half-bull Minotaur, and real Cyclopses—with real thunderbolts—showed up.

"You know what I think?" I said. "I think we should make like a drum—and beat it."

FIVE

We flew across the earth, up a jagged mountainside, and into the clouds in a second. We found ourselves standing in a glowing misty throne room.

"Mount Olympus," said Hera.

Fred, Sam, and I gasped in one voice, "Wow."

We had tried to imagine what Mount Olympus might look like when we built the set for our play, but this place was way beyond our imagination. Golden light and warmth filled the air. White mist swirled everywhere. Eleven robed people stood talking in groups. Twelve thrones lined the room.

"Wait here while I go gather the gods and goddesses," said Hera. "And don't touch anything. You break it, you bought it." She laughed at her own joke and walked over to the other gods.

We stared at the incredible thrones. Each was

different. The biggest one had an emblem of an eagle clutching jagged thunderbolts.

"Our man Zeus's seat," whispered Sam.

The throne next to it was covered with carvings of horse heads and waves.

"His brother Poseidon," said Sam.

The next was all fancy gold and jewels and iron-work.

"Hephaestus, the blacksmith," said Sam.

Next was a fierce-looking vulture's-head throne.

"Ares," continued Sam.

24

"How do you know all this stuff?" asked Fred.

"Fred, if you had a brain, you'd be dangerous," answered Sam. "We've only been studying this stuff and writing it into the play for the last two months."

Fred whacked Sam with his thunderbolt.

"Knock it off, you guys," I said. "We may need that thunderbolt to find *The Book* and get out of here."

"We're going to need a little more magic than this," said Fred, holding up his bent thunderbolt.

Sam named the throne with a lyre, the one with a winged staff, and the last in the row, with bunches of grapes. "Apollo, Hermes, and Dionysus."

"And the other side must be the goddesses' thrones—just like our set," I said.

"Yep," said Sam. And he named the thrones like it was a quiz. "Peacock throne—Hera. Wheat and fruit—Demeter. Owl—Athena. Dove—Aphrodite. Moon—Artemis. Hestia doesn't have a throne. She takes care of the charcoal fire over there."

"Congratulations," said Fred. "Now do you want a medal or a chest to pin it on?"

"Right this way, divine ones," said Hera, leading everyone over to us. "I have some new talent I would like you to meet."

The gods and goddesses drifted over around Hera's throne. Sam nervously adjusted his glasses. Fred straightened his thunderbolt and tried to look tough. I hid the golden apple behind my back.

"Olympians," said Hera, "I want you to meet this trio of very charming beings I just met down on Earth. This is Sam Orpheus, friend of Nike . . ."

Sam bowed and strummed his lyre.

"Fred Cyclops, follower of Reebok . . ."

Fred lifted his thunderbolt and flexed his arm.

"And Joe Paris, cohort of Fila."

I nodded and kept both hands behind my back.

"Please introduce yourselves to our guests," said Hera to the Olympians.

An angry-looking man with a trident stepped forward. "Poseidon, god of the sea. And I should be king of this bunch, but that no-good brother of mine tricked me."

"I'm Demeter, goddess of crops," said a woman holding a bundle of wheat.

The ugliest guy there took a limping step forward holding a giant hammer. "Hephaestus, god of blacksmiths and the working man and—"

26

"And lucky for him, husband to me, Aphrodite, the goddess of love," said a voice like honey.

I looked over and saw the most beautiful woman I had ever seen. I suddenly went all hot. My head buzzed. My heart pounded. The room started to spin.

"Oh, turn off the Love Rays for a minute, would you?" said a goddess carrying a bow. "Call me Artemis, goddess of the hunt."

"A hunt? A fight? I'm there, sir! Ares, sir! God of war, sir!" A tough-looking guy wearing a metal helmet waved his blood-stained spear from side to side. He winked at Aphrodite. "Let me at 'em. I'll rip their heads off. I'll slice their guts out. I'll—"

"Apollo," said a young fellow with a soft voice, ignoring Ares. "Twin brother of Artemis. God of music, poetry, and medicine."

"You're so weak, you couldn't lick a lollipop," said Ares.

"You're certainly strong," said Apollo. "But bad breath isn't everything."

"If you can't say something nice, don't say anything at all," said another goddess.

Sam nudged me. "Hey, check it out. She sounds just like your mom."

I looked again. There was something spookily familiar about her.

"I'm Hestia, goddess of the hearth and home."

"Nah," I said. "She just sounds like everybody's mom."

"Hermes, messenger god of travelers, merchants, bankers, and thieves," said a guy with wings on his sandals.

"Athena," said a woman holding an owl. "Goddess of wisdom and—"

"And PAR-TY!" sang out a wild little guy dressed mostly in vines. "Di-o-ny-sus! God of wine and party time." Dionysus twirled a quick dance step. Ares rolled his eyes.

Hera looked over the crowd. "There. I think that's all of us . . . all except Hades of course. He stays down in that gloomy underworld he rules."

Sam, Fred, and I shivered at the thought of that nasty place.

"And the supposed king of us all, my husband Zeus, who seems to be better at disappearing than ruling," added Hera in an annoyed tone. "I wonder where he could be?"

Sam looked at Fred and me. We all shrugged our shoulders.

"Well forget Old Thunder Butt," said Hera. "We'll start the party without him."

"You tell him!" called Dionysus. The rest of the gods and goddesses laughed and cheered.

"So entertain us," said Hera.

We looked at the assembled gods and goddesses. They looked at us. There was a long pause.

"Are you talking to us?" said Sam.

"No, I'm talking to myself and you overheard me," laughed Hera. "Of course I'm talking to you."

"Of course," answered Sam, laughing nervously. We all realized we were about to be revealed as the fakes we were.

"A clever trick would be nice," said Athena, goddess of wisdom.

"Something with a good dance beat," shouted Dionysus, god of wine.

"Well, I do know one song," said Sam. He pushed his glasses up on his nose and plucked a quick version of "Twinkle, Twinkle, Little Star" on his lyre.

Dead silence.

"Weak," said Apollo, god of music. "Very weak."

29

"I think we should rip his arms off," said Ares. "What have you got, Thunderbolt Boy?"

"Me?" said Fred. And I think that was the first time I ever saw Fred look more than a little nervous. I think it might have had something to do with the way Ares kept waving around that blood-stained spear.

"Oh, you wouldn't want me to do anything with this thunderbolt," said Fred. "Trust me. Unless you happen to have a thin blue book with silver markings on it. Anyone got a thin blue book?"

Everyone stared at us. This was one tough crowd.

"No, I didn't think so," said Fred. "But that's okay, because for the best trick ever—the guy who got us into this will now get us out of it. Take it away, Joe!"

"This is boring," said Demeter. "Can we go back to our nectar and ambrosia now?"

Hera looked thoroughly annoyed. "Fellows. Tricks please. Don't bore us. You don't want to feel the wrath of the angry gods and goddesses of Mount Olympus."

"No siree," said Sam, pushing me forward. "We positively do not want to feel the wrath of the angry gods and goddesses of Mount Olympus, do we Joe?"

The disappearing quarter trick?

"Throw the bums off the mountain like you did to me," said Hephaestus.

The rubber pencil trick?

"Let's twirl their guts out slowly and listen to them scream," said Ares.

A single bead of sweat trickled down the length of my back.

Fred and Sam looked at me. I faced the not-very-happy gods and goddesses of Mount Olympus. It was a much tougher crowd than Jessica and Cynthia and Max and the rest of our classmate gods and goddesses.

This was a crowd that needed nothing less than an impossible trick.

SIX

Nothing less than an impossible trick. An impossible trick.

I had it.

"I have impossible challenges for you all," I said in my best stage magician's voice. "But I will start slowly with an easy math challenge. Take twelve apples from seventeen apples. How many do you have?"

"Five, of course," said Demeter.

"No, twelve," I said. "You have the twelve you took from the seventeen."

Hermes elbowed Hestia. They both laughed.

"Now a tougher challenge," I continued. "Which is correct? 'Twenty-five and eight *is* thirty-four,' or 'twenty-five and eight *are* thirty-four'?"

"Twenty-five and eight *are* thirty-four," Artemis called out.

"No way, sis," said Apollo. "Twenty-five and eight *is* thirty-four."

The gods and goddesses argued back and forth.

"Is."

"Are."

"Is."

"Are."

"Neither," I said. "Twenty-five and eight is *thirty-three*."

Everyone groaned.

"Now for the most difficult challenge," I said.

"Make Athena figure it out," said Aphrodite. "She's always reminding us she's the goddess of wisdom."

Athena shot Aphrodite a nasty look.

"Okay," I said to Athena. "How much dirt is in a hole two meters wide, two meters long, and two meters deep?"

"You call that a challenge? Child's play." Athena tucked her owl under one arm and gestured with the other. "Two by two by two is eight. There are eight cubic meters of dirt in the hole."

"Zero," I said. "There's no dirt in a hole."

"Haw haw haw," Ares hooted, pounding his spear. "Goddess of wisdom, my eye."

Athena was starting to look a little steamed. I figured I'd better do something quick, or she would be my goddess enemy for life.

"But the final challenge calls for someone strong and brave," I said.

Ares pushed aside Poseidon and Dionysus. "You're looking at him."

"I'll bet I can sit somewhere in this room where you can't."

Fred and Sam looked at me like I might be nuts.

"Nothing to it," said Ares.

I sat on the floor, then stood up.

"Can you sit there?"

Ares sat on the floor, then stood up.

"Easy."

I sat on Zeus's throne, then stood up.

"Can you sit there?"

Fred and Sam looked at me like I was definitely nuts.

Ares sat on Zeus's throne.

"Simple."

I sat on Ares' lap. "Can you sit here?" Then I stood up.

Ares stood up, sat down, stood up, and looked confused.

Athena laughed out loud. "Ares, brave and strong god of war, my eye."

"Hey, that's not fair," said Ares.

"Give me another one."

The gods and goddesses all laughed. We had the crowd going now.

Sam elbowed me. "Nice work."

"Yeah, that was a close one," said Fred, tugging on his Cyclops cap.

"One more trick. Then we get *The Book* and blast out of here," I whispered to Fred. I said, "Okay, Olympians, for Ares' final challenge, I need a coin. Does anyone have a coin?"

Everyone gave me a blank look.

"Coin?" said Hera. "We're gods and goddesses. We live on nectar and ambrosia. We don't have coins."

Dionysus spun and twirled his toga in a circle. "We don't even have pockets, man."

Then I realized I was still holding the apple. "Any object will do. Ares, I'll bet I can put this apple down and you won't be able to jump over it."

"You're not going to put it in my lap?" said Ares.

"I'm not going to put it in your lap," I said.

"Let's go." Ares handed his blood-stained spear to Hestia. "Hold this. I'm jumping over the moon."

I held the apple carefully in two hands. I looked

slowly to the left. I looked slowly to the right. Then I put the apple on top of Ares' head.

Hestia smiled. Dionysus danced. Aphrodite clapped.

"Wonderful," said Poseidon in a watery growl.

"Fantastic," said Sam. "Now let's take a look at that book."

"So clever," said Athena.

"*The Book*?" said Fred.

"Very funny," said Hestia, smoothing my hair just like my mom does.

"Thanks," I said. "But we do have our own Mount Olympus we have to get back to for opening night. So if we could just take a peek at *The Book* and—"

"It's such a shame," said Hera. "Zeus missed everything."

A familiar whoosh of feathers and burst of light filled Mount Olympus. "ZEUS MISSED WHAT?" said Zeus, suddenly appearing on his throne.

"Well look who's here," said Hera. "King Thunderhead. I'm sorry you missed it. The boys have to go. Hestia, do you know where the blue book is?"

"Of course," said Hestia, goddess of home. "It's on the bookshelf."

"NOT SO FAST," thundered Zeus, crackling and shooting off little sparks. He looked a little shocked and frazzled since we saw him last. "Your new friends were going to trade me the book for that thunderbolt there." He pointed to Fred's aluminum foil weapon. "But I just met up with Typhon and a gang of monsters and had a rather *electrifying meeting . . .*" Zeus looked me square in the eye, "if you know what I mean."

I knew what he meant. The jig was up. Just like in our play, Zeus had met the monsters and they had the real thunderbolts. And now he knew we were fakes.

I had a sudden brainstorm. If we could get our hands on *The Book* for even just a second, we could disappear in a puff of green mist before anyone could stop us.

"You know what?" I said. "I just remembered a great trick. Give me *The Book* and I'll show you the best trick of all."

Zeus sat, still smoking and popping from his run-in with the monsters and the thunderbolts.

Hestia came back with something wrapped in a golden cloth.

"Here's the book," she said.

We were home free. I reached for the bundle.

"I don't think so," said Zeus. He took the bundle, looked at me, and smiled a cruel smile. "Why don't you do the trick where you give the golden apple to the goddess it belongs to."

My heart stopped.

"It's for the fairest," said Hera. "It's obviously for me."

"For the fairest?" said Athena. "Obviously me."

"The fairest?" said Aphrodite. "That would be me."

"Who's the fairest?" said Zeus.

I clutched the golden apple. I didn't dare look at Hera, Athena, or Aphrodite. I didn't know who was the fairest. But I did know that this wasn't Sara, Jessica, or Cynthia I was messing with, and no matter which goddess I chose, I would be the deadest.

SEVEN

"Give me the apple," said Hera. "I will give you power and riches."

"Give me the apple," said Athena. "I will give you victories and wisdom."

"Give me the apple," said Aphrodite. "I will give you the love of the most beautiful woman in the world."

I stood in the middle of Mount Olympus, holding a gold spray-painted plastic apple, trapped like a rat. No matter which goddess I chose, I would be in deep trouble with the other two.

Zeus smiled a mean smile. It reminded me of the nasty kind of smile Mr. Snide would give us in history class while he was assigning a monster history project due the day after vacation.

I hefted the apple, thinking. The love of the most

beautiful woman in the world wouldn't do me much good in math class or on the basketball team. So it was down to either Hera or Athena.

I looked at Sam and Fred.

"Pick Hera," said Fred. "You'll be rich forever. Plus, you'll be powerful enough to beat up anybody who doesn't like it."

"Athena is the obvious choice," said Sam. "Brains are what's important. You'll be smart enough to make all the money you want, *and* figure out any problem."

"Well?" said Zeus. "Come on, already. Who's the fairest?"

Fred's argument made some sense. But Sam's made more sense. I could give the apple to Athena, get wisdom, and then figure out how to get us out of this Greek myth jam without getting fried by Zeus or torn to shreds by two angry goddesses.

I held the apple out in front of me. "The golden apple goes to—"

I looked at Hera. I started to give the apple to Athena. But then I looked at Aphrodite. She smiled. My heart stopped beating for a second. A hot wave washed over my head. Voices and sounds rushed to a pinpoint roaring in my ears. I was in love.

"The app . . . ulll . . . goth . . . to . . ." I couldn't talk. I couldn't think. I stumbled through my fog toward Aphrodite.

"She's cheating!" yelled Athena. "She's using her Love Ray again."

Something whacked me on the back of my head. It was Ares, Aphrodite's boyfriend. He was not happy, and he was getting ready to whack me again. That was too much for Fred.

Now Fred is one of those guys who gets a lot of comments in his school reports about "self control" and "focus." But you know what I like about

42

Fred? If he sees one of his friends in trouble, he jumps right into the rumble. And that's exactly what he did to save me on Mount Olympus.

Fred threw down his thunderbolt. He hopped onto the arm of Hera's throne and launched himself into the air. He yelled a crazy Tarzan kind of yell, landed on Ares' shoulders, and wrapped his arms around Ares' helmeted head.

Ares swung around blindly, slicing off the tip of Zeus's beard with his spear.

Zeus roared. Dionysus screamed.

Ares, still blinded by Fred's arms, swung his spear in dangerous circles. Artemis dodged the sharp tip and tried to pull Fred off Ares. Apollo dove and grabbed Artemis to save her. Ares swung in another wobbly circle and sliced a pillow in half. I saw an opening and threw a cross body check on him.

The whole pile of Ares, Fred, Artemis, and Apollo crashed into Zeus's lap. *The Book* flew one way. The golden apple flew the other. Before anyone else could move, Sam saw his chance and jumped on the cloth-wrapped book.

"I've got it!" yelled Sam.

Everyone looked at Sam in surprise.

He fumbled with the cloth and quickly unwrapped the thin blue book. He held it up. "Home sweet home . . . home sweet home . . ."

But something was wrong. There was no green time-traveling mist. We were still on Mount Olympus. And we were still surrounded by a bunch of very angry gods and goddesses.

Sam looked at the book closely. I looked at Sam, and I knew something was very wrong.

EIGHT

Sam read the cover of the book. *"The Little Blue Book of Insults?"*

"What were you expecting?" said Hera. "The Yellow Pages? You asked for the blue book. I told you I use it every day. It's where I get all my best insults."

"Oh no," groaned Sam.

"Oh yes," said a mad-looking Zeus. He stood up and straightened his robes. "No more stalling. Joe Paris—award that apple and let's start the fireworks."

Fred and I untangled ourselves from Ares, Artemis, and Apollo. I walked slowly over to pick up the golden apple, thinking, "I'm doomed. Doomed as doomed can be."

The apple had rolled over into a corner of the

throne room. I bent over to pick it up and bumped my head against the wall.

And that's what gave me my brilliant idea.

"That's it," I said. "I've got it."

"You'd better get it," said Zeus. "Otherwise I'm going to start frying you and your friends."

I held the apple in front of me. "I will award the apple to the god or goddess who can meet my simple challenge of jumping over it when I put it on the floor," I said. "If no one meets the challenge, you have to give us nectar and ambrosia, make us gods, *and* help us find our book."

Zeus looked confused. "All we have to do is jump over the apple?"

"All you have to do is jump over the apple," I repeated.

"No putting it on anybody's head this time," said Ares.

"No putting it on anybody's head," I promised.

"I'm the queen, so I go first," said Hera. "That apple is as good as mine."

"No, as goddess of wisdom, I should go first," said Athena.

"Me first," said Poseidon. "I'm older."

"Me," said Hermes. "I can run faster and jump higher than any of you."

"Give me a chance at something for once," said the lame Hephaestus.

"I'm Zeus and what I say goes!—me first."

Everyone started talking and yelling at once. It looked like another brawl was going to break out when a calm voice spoke up.

"Olympians," said Hestia, in her mom-like voice. "Everyone can take a turn. We'll go in alphabetical order."

Everyone calmed down, mumbling and grumbling. Athena was the first to figure out the alphabetical order. She frowned. "Why does it always have to be Miss Airhead?"

"I get to go first?" said Aphrodite sweetly.

"Well gosh, no. I thought Zeus got to go first," said Hera meanly.

"Okay, okay. Let's get on with the challenge already," said Zeus. "But this better be good . . . or else."

Fred picked up his thunderbolt looking a bit worried.

Sam tugged at his toga looking very worried.

"Are we sure we want to do this, Joe Paris?"

"Yes we do, Sam Orpheus," I said. I held the apple up in one hand. "The golden apple will be awarded to whoever can jump over it. Follow me." I walked over to where I had retrieved the apple and got the idea. I put it on the floor snugly in the corner. Everyone stared. It was impossible for anyone to jump over it.

There was a pause.

Fred and Sam let out a yell. "Yes!"

Ares pounded the floor angrily with his spear.

Athena, Hera, and Aphrodite looked disappointed that not one of them would get the apple. Zeus looked puzzled again. Hestia smiled and nodded.

Dionysus took a drink of his wine and let out one long loud laugh. "He got us. Fair and square. Nobody's jumping that golden apple. Bring out the nectar and ambrosia."

Sam and Fred pounded me on the back. We had done it. We were as good as back at school for the opening of the play *and* we were going to be coming back as real gods. Who could ask for a happier ending?

We would have celebrated more, but we heard a sound that cut things short. It was that familiar sound. The sound of tromping feet, one voice calling, and a crowd of ugly voices answering.

It was the sound of the hundred-dragon-headed Typhon and the monsters of Greek mythology marching into Mount Olympus with a really nasty trick—Zeus's missing thunderbolts.

NINE

We are monsters like no other.
WE ARE MONSTERS LIKE NO OTHER.
We will stomp you and your mother.
WE WILL STOMP YOU
AND YOUR MOTHER.
Sound off!
MON—STERS!
Say it again!
MON—STERS!
Bring it on down!
MONSTERS, MONSTERS, MONSTERS
WE RULE!

Typhon and his monster pals filled half the throne room. Fred, Sam, and I and all the gods and goddesses gathered together by the thrones in the other half.

Typhon himself was the weirdest, scariest thing I've ever seen. In the play, Brian dressed up as Typhon by pinning a lot of extra paper-plate heads on his costume. But the real thing was unbelievable. One hundred heads on thick snaking necks sprouted out of Typhon's shoulders. Heads shaped like dragons, bulls, tigers, lions, and unnameable things roared and hissed and screamed and yowled.

Sam's eyes bugged out, and he fell back on Hera's throne. He looked so white, I thought he had fainted.

Behind Typhon, that guy named Geryon with three bodies and one head held our old friend three-headed Cerberus on a leash. Huge birds with razor-sharp claws and women's heads swooped through the air. A pack of the real giant one-eyed Cyclops guys crowded a group of scaly-skinned women with snakes for hair. The half-man half-bull Minotaur led a goat-and-lion-headed beast with a giant snake-head tail. Mount Olympus smoked red and black with poisonous heat and noise.

"I see it, but I don't believe it," breathed Fred.

"Believe it," said Sam. "And don't look into the eyes of those snake-haired women. They're gorgons, and one of them's Medusa. One look from her will turn you to stone."

I turned to check out Zeus. He looked about as happy as Sam to see this bunch.

"Now just a fire-breathing minute," said Hera. "This is Mount Olympus. What do all you monsters think you are doing bursting in here like this? You turn around and march right back down to your caves or mazes or underground holes or wherever it is you live, and don't let me see you messing around up here again or Zeus will give you a mighty thrashing and a blast of his thunderbolts. Isn't that right, dear?"

Zeus didn't say a word.

Typhon's hundred heads hissed and bellowed and squealed. Then one bright red human head right in the middle of the whole mess spoke up.

"Thank you for that warm welcome, Hera. But we plan to stay. In fact, we monsters are taking over Mount Olympus!"

The flying woman-headed harpies screeched and laughed, dive bombing our heads.

"And I don't think Zeus is going to be blasting anyone with his mighty thunderbolts," hissed Typhon's red head. Then he threw something into the air that shook the stars with a sonic boom.

Cerberus howled.

The monsters cheered.

"Typhon has Zeus's thunderbolts," said Athena.

"Brilliant observation, goddess of wisdom," said Aphrodite.

"Clean out your thrones and hit the road," said Typhon. "Monsters rule!"

"In your dreams Hundred Head," said Ares. "I'm the god of war and I'll fight you for it."

The gang of Cyclopses chanted together, "Lean to the left. Lean to the right. Cyclops! Cyclops! Fight fight fight!"

Fred nudged me. "That's my line. That's exactly my Cyclops line from the play."

"I know. I know," I said. "The only problem is, it's not Brian and David and Charlie we're facing. It's the real Typhon, the real Cyclopses, and the real thunderbolts."

Artemis notched an arrow in her bow and drew it back. Poseidon raised his barbed trident. The three-headed fire-breathing Chimera hissed with its snake head, bleated with its goat head, and roared with its lion head all at once. Ares waved his spear. The Cyclopses picked up giant rocks.

Both sides stood ready to charge.

Sam held his lyre over his head. "Someone could get hurt."

Zeus turned suddenly and grabbed Fred's thunderbolt.

"Well you didn't get all the thunderbolts, smart guy. Die, Typhon, die!"

And Zeus hurled the thunderbolt with all his might.

It flew like a shot and nailed Typhon right in the middle of his red human head.

Monsters, gods, and goddesses froze.

Fred's aluminum-foil-covered thunderbolt bounced off Typhon's forehead and fell harmlessly to the ground. Typhon looked down at the prop thunderbolt with the now-broken tip. He looked up and smiled a very evil smile.

"Someone is definitely going to get hurt," said Sam.

TEN

About one second after Fred's thunderbolt hit the ground, all Hades broke loose.

The Minotaur charged. Dionysus vaulted over his horns and hung on for dear life. Poseidon pinned the Chimera's snake-head tail to the ground, but its nasty goat head butted him flying. Lightning and thunder rocked the air. Sam, Fred, and I dove under Zeus's overturned throne.

"Joe, this is completely out of control," said Sam. "If the monsters take over Mount Olympus, all the stories of the Greek myths will be changed, and I think we will be in a whole lot of permanent trouble."

"Can't you do one of those big exploding puff-of-smoke tricks like your uncle Joe does?" said Fred.

I peeked out and saw Hera pulling a gorgon's snake hair. Athena twirled her sword over her head to fight off three nagging harpies.

"I don't think this crowd is really in the mood for tricks," I said. "We've got to find *The Book* to get Greek mythology back to normal and us back to school. So why don't we—"

"Ahhhh!" screamed Sam.

One of Typhon's dragon heads scooped Sam up in its jaws and dragged him out from under the throne. Fred and I both grabbed for his foot . . . but he was gone. We jumped out into the battle to see Sam bonk the dragon head with his lyre. It made a musical *boinnnnggg*. The dragon head paused to listen.

That gave me the plan. Our play had brought the Greek myths to life. Maybe something from the play could save our lives.

"Hit it again!" I yelled.

"Are you crazy?" said Fred. "You're just going to make it madder."

Sam's lyre gave another *boinnnnggg*.

"Not the dragon head!" I yelled. "Hit the *lyre,* Sam."

Two of Typhon's other heads turned toward the musical noise.

"Music is the power. Just like in the play. Play some music to conquer these monsters," I called.

"I hope you know what you're doing," said Fred.

"Me too," I said. Because if not, Sam was dragon lunch.

Sam strummed a few notes. Two of the harpies fluttered down onto Aphrodite's throne to listen.

"Go, Sam go," said Fred. "I think it's working."

The dragon head lowered Sam to the ground. He started his one and only song again—"Twinkle, Twinkle, Little Star." Hera and the gorgons stopped to listen. A few more bars, and the Minotaur looked up. All three of Cerberus's heads turned Sam's way.

"But he only knows one song," whispered Fred. "As soon as they figure that out, we're cooked."

The sound of the

lyre slowly overtook the screams and shouts of fighting.

"If we could only find someone who could play more," I said. "But who . . . ?"

"Apollo," said a voice in my ear.

"Apollo!" I said. "Of course! The god of music. Who else?" I turned around, and there was Hestia. It was her voice. She pointed to Apollo, who was helping Artemis fight off three rock-crushing Cyclopses. I hopped over a stream of poisonous burning Cerberus drool and dodged my way over there.

"Apollo," I said. "You're our only hope. Can you play anything besides 'Twinkle, Twinkle, Little Star'?"

Apollo ducked under a Cyclops' swinging fist. He looked at me like I was from the moon. "Can I play music? Is Aphrodite beautiful? Is Athena smart? Can Dionysus drink wine? Hand me that stringed thing. I'll show you music."

"Sam," I called. "Hand the lyre over to Apollo."

Sam backed up toward us slowly. The eyes of Typhon, the gorgons, and half the harpies were on him.

"Be my guest," said Sam. He stopped in mid-verse, tossed the lyre to Apollo, and dove behind Hestia.

Apollo caught the lyre and finished the song without missing a beat.

Cerberus growled a warning.

One of the harpies squawked.

Apollo started "Twinkle, Twinkle" again, but this time he turned it into a wild waterfall of notes playing over, around, and through the tune.

The snakes on the gorgons' heads started swaying with the music. The Cyclopses stomped their big ugly feet in time. Zeus and Hera rocked, with their arms around each other.

I couldn't believe it. It was just like in our play. Music was the answer to calm the crazy monsters and all the fighting gods and goddesses.

Apollo must have played ten different variations on "Twinkle, Twinkle, Little Star," each more amazing than the last. Every one of the gods and monsters was hypnotized by the sound.

I looked around Mount Olympus. Aphrodite held Typhon's hand. Dionysus danced with the Minotaur. Everybody was happy. Everybody but

Fred, Sam, and me. The gods and monsters of Greek mythology were safe, but we were still three guys in bed-sheet togas a long way from home.

I felt an arm around my shoulder. It was Hestia. "You knew the answer to save us all along," she said.

"I guess we did," I said. "I just wish we knew the answer to save ourselves."

"And get us back to opening night," said Sam.

Fred picked up his broken thunderbolt and knocked it thoughtfully against his own head. "It might not be bad to hang out and be gods for a while."

"Yeah," said Sam, not very convincingly.

"I'd give it all up for *The Book*," I said.

"Done," said Hestia. She held up a small blue book wrapped in gold cloth.

"No more insults," said Sam. "I think even I've had enough for one day."

Hestia handed me my slightly scuffed golden apple. "Here, you'll need this." She straightened my toga with a gentle pat. "Break a leg." She handed me the half-wrapped book and touched Fred's thunderbolt to it. Something sparked and glowed

weirdly for a second. Then a wisp of green mist swirled around us.

"A book! Our book! It's not a book, it's *The Book!*" babbled Sam.

I looked down at the thin blue book covered with odd silver writing and symbols. "But how—? Who—? Where—?" I stuttered.

Hestia smiled a very mom-like smile. "I told you

it was on the bookshelf. I guess it always takes the goddess of hearth and home to find things around here."

The green mist spun around us. We floated over the peaceful gods and monsters wrapped in the sound of Apollo's song and disappeared into time, space, and who knows where.

ELEVEN

Music washed over everyone. Gods and monsters danced arm in arm. And then it was over. The lights faded to black.

The parents stood and clapped and cheered. We bowed. Fred launched his slightly battered thunderbolt out over the crowd. The audience clapped and cheered more, and more, and more.

Opening night was a smashing success.

After everyone got changed backstage, Fred, Sam, and I found our parents in the crowd outside the auditorium. The moms looked at us all misty eyed. The dads patted us on the back.

"You were wonderful," said Sam's mom.

"Just like we were really there on Mount Olympus," said Fred's dad.

Fred, Sam, and I looked at each other.

"You can say that again," said Fred.

I took a certain thin blue book wrapped in gold cloth out of my backpack. "Where's Uncle Joe? I have something I have to give him."

"Oh, he disappeared like he always does," said my mom. "I'm not sure where he went."

"Oh great," I said.

"Is it something I could take?" My mom put her arm around me exactly like Hestia had on Mount Olympus.

"I . . . uhh . . ."

Sam nodded his head up and down.

"Well, I think . . ."

Fred gave me a quick thumbs-up sign.

I thought about all the trouble *The Book* had got us into. I thought about the great adventures *The Book* had got us into.

I tucked the golden package carefully back into my backpack.

Sam and Fred stared at me in disbelief.

"I think I'll just hang on to it . . . and figure out another plan."

THE MYTH OF POWER
Our School Play About Greek Mythology

CAST
GODS AND GODDESSES/OLYMPIANS

Zeus (ZŪS):   Most powerful of the gods.
                            Ruler of gods and mortals.

Hera (HIR-a):   Queen of the gods. Married to
                            Zeus.

Aphrodite (af-ro-DĪ-tē):   Goddess of love and beauty,
                            and she knows it.

Apollo (a-POL-ō):   The sun god and god of the
                            fine arts. Son of Zeus. Twin
                            brother of Artemis.

Ares (Ā-rēs):   God of war. Son of Zeus.
                            Always looking for a fight.

Artemis (AR-te-mis):   The moon goddess and god-
                            dess of hunting. Daughter of
                            Zeus. Twin sister of Apollo.

Athena (a-THĒ-na):   Goddess of wisdom, born fully
                            formed out of the head of
                            Zeus. Ouch.

Demeter (de-MĒ-ter):   Goddess of agriculture. Sister
                            of Zeus. Lost her daughter

Persephone to Hades.

Dionysus (dī-o-NĪ-sus):   God of wine. Son of Zeus.
                            Threw the original toga party.

Hades (HĀ-dēz):   Ruler of the underworld,
                            which is called by his name.
                            Brother of Zeus.

Hephaestus (he-FES-tus):   The blacksmith god. Son of
                            Hera and Zeus. Husband of
                            Aphrodite. Tossed off Mount
                            Olympus by Hera because he
                            was so ugly.

Hermes (HER-mēz):   Messenger of the gods. Son of
                            Zeus. Fast on his feet.

Hestia (HES-ti-a):   Goddess of the household.
                            Older sister of Zeus. She
                            didn't have a throne, but no
                            one messed with her.

Poseidon (po-SĪ-don):   God of the sea. Another broth-
                            er in that happy Zeus, Hades,
                            Demeter, Hera, Hestia family.

MONSTERS

Typhon (TĪ-fon):   Hundred-headed flame-
                            breathing leader of the monsters.

Cerberus (SER-ber-us): Three-headed guard dog of Hades.

Cyclopses (SĪ-klop-sez) Unpleasant giant one-eyed guys.

Medusa (me-DŪ-sa): Most famous of the gorgons (see below).

Chimera (kī-MĒ-ra): Fire-breathing beast with the head of a lion, body of a goat, and tail of a snake. Lovely.

Harpies (HAR-pēz): Fierce, smelly, winged things with the faces of women, bodies of vultures, and nagging ways.

Geryon (JER-i-on): Three bodies, one head, and we're still not sure how he did it.

Griffins (GRIF-inz): Half eagle, half lion, all nasty.

Gorgons (GOR-gonz): Three women with snakes for hair, and a look that could turn you to stone.

Minotaur (MI-no-tor): Half-man, half-bull. Kept in a labyrinth. And you thought you had problems.

MAKE YOUR OWN
GREEK MYTHOLOGY PROPS

Orpheus's Lyre

1. Get a flexible stick.
2. Bend it into a U shape.
3. String rubber bands across the U.
4. Play "Three Blind Mice" over and over until everyone begs you to stop.

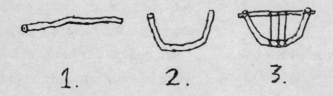

1. 2. 3.

Zeus's Thunderbolt

1. Cut cardboard into the shape of a thunderbolt.
2. Cover with aluminum foil.
3. Destroy all monsters. Amaze your friends.

1. 2.

Paris's Golden Apple

1. Find one plastic apple.
2. Spray paint it gold.
3. Award it to "The Fairest"
4. Run for your life from the mad losers who don't win the apple.

1.   2.

For a free copy of the complete text of the play
The Myth of Power (written by Jon for
his daughter's fourth grade class) visit the
Jon Scieszka and Lane Smith website at:
http://www.chucklebait.com

Break a leg.